For OGF, with love
Bernette Ford

For Boxer Books
Sam Williams

First American edition published in 2006
by Boxer Books Limited.

Distributed in the United States and Canada by
Sterling Publishing Co., Inc.
387 Park Avenue South, New York, NY 10016-8810

First published in Great Britain in 2006
by Boxer Books Limited.
www.boxerbooks.com

ISBN 10: 1-905417-33-0
ISBN 13: 978-1-905417-33-9

Printed in China

# No More Diapers
## for
## Ducky!

Bernette Ford and Sam Williams

Boxer Books

Ducky knocks on Piggy's door.

No one answers.

"Come out, Piggy," she calls.

"Come out and play with me."

Piggy is busy.

"I can't come out now," he calls.

"I am sitting on the potty!"

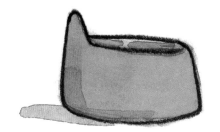

Ducky goes inside.

She goes into Piggy's room.

She plays with Piggy's toys.

She reads Piggy's books.

Ducky knocks on the bathroom door.

"Can't you come out now?" she asks.

Piggy looks up from his book.

"I told you,"

he says through the door.

"I am sitting on the potty."

Ducky wears a diaper.

It feels cold.

It feels wet.

Ducky wriggles out

of her diaper.

She kicks her diaper

across the floor.

Knock, knock, knock!

"Let me in," says Ducky.

"I have to use the potty."

"You wear diapers!" says Piggy.

"Not anymore," says Ducky.

"No more diapers for Ducky!"

Piggy pulls up his pants.

He washes his hands.

He opens the door.

He lets Ducky into the bathroom.

Now Piggy plays with his toys.

He reads his books.

After a while, he calls,

"Come out and play, Ducky."

"I can't play now," says Ducky.

"I am sitting on the potty!"